My dar

Antho

with

first

Mam
X

My first book of...
Nursery Rhymes & Poems

Previously published as:
My First Book of Nursery Rhymes
by Tiger Books International in 1988
My First Book of Poems
by Tiger Books International in 1989

This edition published in 2010 by Chancellor Press,
an imprint of Octopus Publishing Group Ltd

An Hachette UK Company
www.hachette.co.uk

Reprinted 2011

Copyright © 2005 Octopus Publishing Group Ltd

ISBN: 978-0-753720-47-9

A CIP catalogue record for this book is available from the British Library

Printed and bound in China

My first book of...

Nursery Rhymes & Poems

CHANCELLOR
PRESS

CONTENTS
NURSERY RHYMES

CONTENTS

POEMS

LITTLE MISS MUFFET

Little Miss Muffet
Sat on a tuffet,
Eating her curds and whey.
There came a big spider,
Who sat down beside her
And frightened Miss Muffet away.

OLD MOTHER HUBBARD

Old Mother Hubbard,
Went to the cupboard,
To fetch her poor dog a bone.
But when she got there,
The cupboard was bare,
And so the poor dog had none.

The dame made a curtsey,
The dog made a bow.
The dame said, "Your servant,"
The dog said, "Bow-wow."

JACK AND JILL

Jack and Jill went up the hill
To fetch a pail of water.
Jack fell down and broke his crown
And Jill came tumbling after.

Up Jack got and home did trot
As fast as he could caper.
He went to bed and wrapped his head
In vinegar and brown paper.

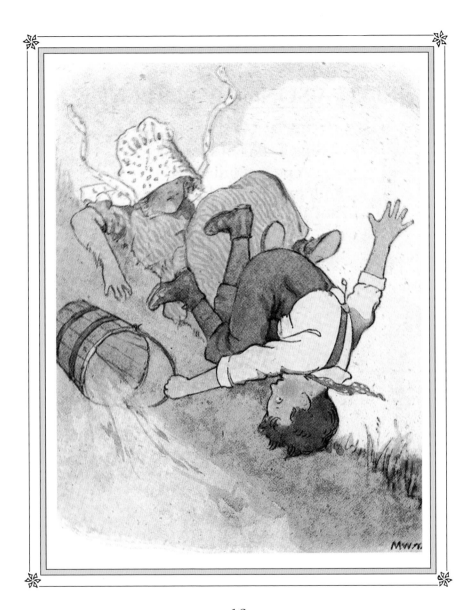

SING A SONG OF SIXPENCE

Sing a song of sixpence,
A pocket full of rye.
Four and twenty blackbirds,
Baked in a pie!

When the pie was opened,
The birds began to sing.
Wasn't that a dainty dish,
To set before the king?

The king was in his counting house,
Counting out his money.
The queen was in the parlour,
Eating bread and honey.

The maid was in the garden,
Hanging out the clothes,
When down came a blackbird
And pecked off her nose!

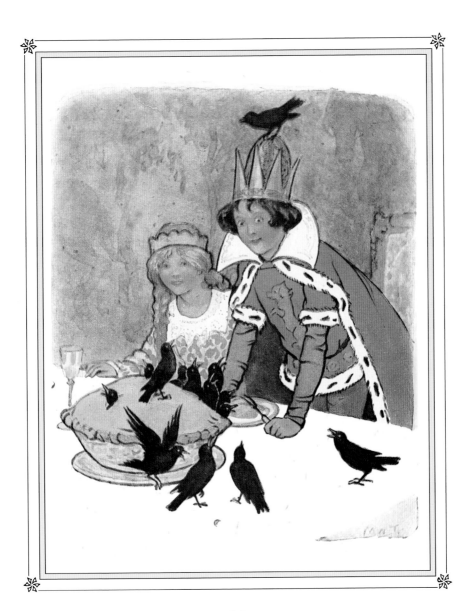

LITTLE BO-PEEP

Little Bo-peep has lost her sheep,
And doesn't know where to find them.
Leave them alone, and they'll come home,
Wagging their tails behind them.

HUMPTY DUMPTY

Humpty Dumpty sat on the wall,
Humpty Dumpty had a great fall.
All the king's horses and all the king's men,
Couldn't put Humpty together again!

BAA, BAA, BLACK SHEEP

Baa, baa, black sheep,
Have you any wool?

Yes Sir, yes Sir,
Three bags full.

One for my master,
And one for my dame.

And one for the little boy
Who lives down the lane.

WHERE ARE YOU GOING?

"Where are you going, my pretty maid?"
"I'm going a-milking, Sir," she said,
"Sir," she said, "Sir," she said.
"I'm going a-milking, Sir," she said.

"What is your fortune, my pretty maid?"
"My face is my fortune, Sir," she said,
"Sir," she said, "Sir," she said.
"My face is my fortune, Sir," she said.

"Then I can't marry you, my pretty maid."
"Nobody asked you, Sir," she said.
"Sir," she said, "Sir," she said.
"Nobody asked you, Sir," she said.

OLD KING COLE

Old King Cole
Was a merry old soul,
And a merry old soul was he.
He called for his pipe,
And he called for his bowl,
And he called for his fiddlers three.

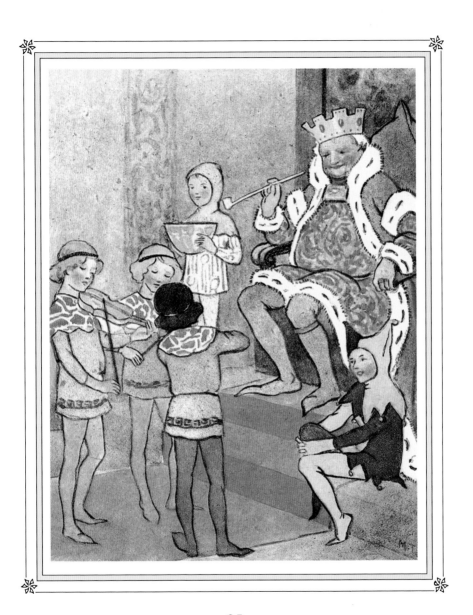

PEASE PORRIDGE HOT

Pease porridge hot,
Pease porridge cold,
Pease porridge in the pot
Nine days old.

Some like it hot,
Some like it cold,
Some like it in the pot
Nine days old.

JACK SPRAT

Jack Sprat could eat no fat,
His wife could eat no lean,
And so between them both, you see,
They licked the platter clean.

RUB-A-DUB-DUB

Rub-a-dub-dub,
Three men in a tub,
And how do you think they got there?
The butcher, the baker,
The candlestick maker,
They all jumped out of a rotten potato,
'Twas enough to make a man stare.

RIDE A COCK HORSE

Ride a cock horse to Banbury Cross,
To see a fine lady upon a white horse.
With rings on her fingers,
And bells on her toes,
She shall have music wherever she goes.

LITTLE TOMMY TUCKER

Little Tommy Tucker
Sings for his supper.
What shall we give him?
Brown bread and butter.
How will he cut it
Without a knife?
How can he marry
Without e'er a wife?

DING DONG BELL

Ding dong bell,
Pussy's in the well.
Who put her in?
Little Johnny Green.
Who pulled her out?
Little Tommy Stout.

What a naughty boy was that
To try and drown poor pussy cat,
Who never did any harm,
But killed all the mice
In his father's barn.

BYE, BABY BUNTING

Bye, baby bunting,
Daddy's gone a-hunting,
To get a little rabbit's skin
To wrap his baby bunting in.

LITTLE BOY BLUE

Little Boy Blue
Come blow your horn!
The sheep's in the meadow,
The cow's in the corn!

Where is the boy
Who looks after the sheep?
He's under the haystack
Fast asleep!

Will you wake him?
No, not I,
For if I do,
He's sure to cry.

SIMPLE SIMON

Simple Simon met a pieman
Going to the fair.
Said Simple Simon to the pieman,
"Please let me taste your ware."

Said the pieman to Simple Simon
"Show me first your penny."
Said Simple Simon to the pieman,
"Indeed I have not any."

Simple Simon went a-fishing,
For to catch a whale.
All the water he had got
Was in his mother's pail!

Simple Simon went to look
If plums grew on a thistle.
He pricked his finger very much,
Which made poor Simon whistle!

MARY, MARY, QUITE CONTRARY

Mary, Mary, quite contrary,
How does your garden grow?
With silver bells and cockle shells,
And pretty maids all in a row, row, row,
And pretty maids all in a row.

HEY DIDDLE-DIDDLE

Hey diddle-diddle,
The cat and the fiddle,
The cow jumped over the moon.
The little boy laughed
To see such fun,
And the dish ran away with the spoon!

WEE WILLIE WINKIE

Wee Willie Winkie
Runs through the town,
Upstairs and downstairs,
In his nightgown.

Calling through the window,
Crying through the lock,
"Are all the children in their beds?
It's after eight o'clock!"

HICKORY, DICKORY, DOCK

Hickory, dickory, dock!
The mouse ran up the clock.
The clock struck one,
The mouse ran down,
Hickory, dickory, dock.

GEORGIE PORGIE

Georgie Porgie, pudding and pie,
Kissed the girls and made them cry.
When the boys came out to play,
Georgie Porgie ran away.

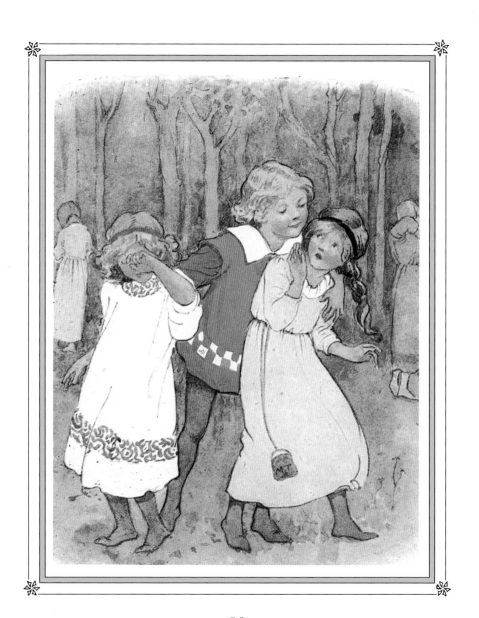

TOM, TOM, THE PIPER'S SON

Tom, Tom, the piper's son,
Stole a pig and away did run.
The pig was eat, and Tom was beat,
And Tom went crying down the street.

RING-A-RING O' ROSES

Ring-a-ring o' roses,
A pocket full of posies,
A-tishoo! A-tishoo!
We all fall down.

THIS LITTLE PIG

This little pig went to market,
This little pig stayed at home,
This little pig had roast beef,
But this little pig had none,
And this little pig cried,
"Wee, wee, wee,
All the way home!"

THE QUEEN OF HEARTS

The Queen of Hearts,
She made some tarts,
All on a summer's day.
The Knave of Hearts,
He stole the tarts,
And took them clean away.

The King of Hearts,
Called for the tarts,
And beat the Knave full sore.
The Knave of Hearts
Brought back the tarts,
And vowed he'd steal no more.

HUSH-A-BYE BABY

Hush-a-bye baby,
On the tree top.
When the wind blows,
The cradle will rock.
When the bough breaks
The cradle will fall,
And down will come baby,
Cradle and all.

POLLY, PUT THE KETTLE ON

Polly, put the kettle on,
Polly, put the kettle on,
Polly, put the kettle on,
    We'll all have tea.

Sally, take it off again,
Sally, take it off again,
Sally, take it off again,
They've all gone away.

POEMS

THE LAND OF COUNTERPANE

When I was sick and lay a-bed,
I had two pillows at my head,
And all my toys beside me lay
To keep me happy all the day.

And sometimes for an hour or so
I watched my leaden soldiers go,
With different uniforms and drills,
Among the bedclothes, through the hills;

And sometimes sent my ships in fleets
All up and down among the sheets;
Or brought my trees and houses out,
And planted cities all about.

I was the giant great and still
That sits upon the pillow-hill,
And sees before him, dale and plain,
The pleasant land of counterpane.

Robert Louis Stevenson

COME UNTO THESE YELLOW SANDS

Come unto these yellow sands,
And then take hands:
Curtsied when you have and kiss'd,
The wild waves whist,
Foot it featly here and there;
And, sweet sprites, the burden bear.
Hark, hark!
Bow wow
The watch-dogs bark:
Bow wow
Hark, hark! I hear
The strain of strutting chanticleer
Cry, *Cock-a-diddle-dow.*

William Shakespeare

CHILD'S SONG IN SPRING

The silver birch is a dainty lady,
    She wears a satin gown;
The elm tree makes the old churchyard shady,
    He will not live in town.

The English oak is a sturdy fellow,
    He gets his green coat late;
The willow is smart in a suit of yellow,
    While the brown beech trees wait.

Such a gay green gown God gives the larches—
    As green as He is good!
The hazels hold up their arms for arches
    When Spring rides through the wood.

The chestnut's proud and the lilac's pretty,
    The poplar's gentle and tall,
But the plane tree is kind to the poor dull city—
    I love him best of all!

F. Nesbit

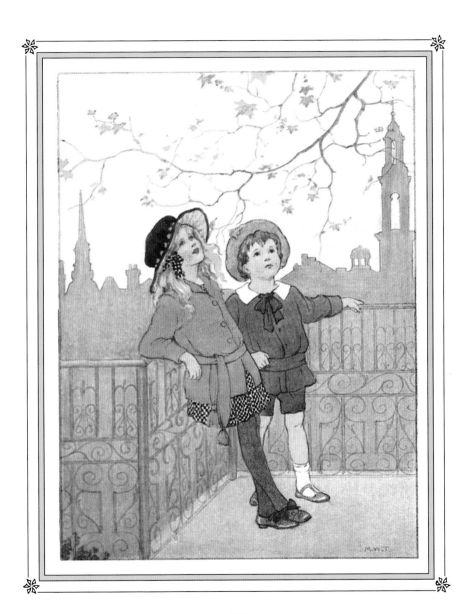

BUBBLE-BLOWING

Our plot is small, but sunny limes
    Shut out all cares and troubles;
And there my little girl at times
    And I sit blowing bubbles.

They glide, they dart, they soar, they break.
    Oh, joyous little daughter,
What lovely coloured worlds we make,
    What crystal flowers of water!

One, green and rosy, slowly drops;
    One soars and shines a minute,
And carries to the lime tree tops
    Our home, reflected in it.

To her enchanted with the gleam,
    The glamour and the glory,
The bubble home's a home of dream,
    And I must tell its story.

William Canton

WYNKEN, BLYNKEN, AND NOD

Wynken, Blynken, and Nod one night
   Sailed off in a wooden shoe,—
Sailed on a river of crystal light
   Into a sea of dew.
"Where are you going, and what do you wish?"
   The old moon asked the three.
"We have come to fish for the herring fish
   That live in this beautiful sea;
Nets of silver and gold have we,"

       Said Wynken,
       Blynken,
       And Nod.

continued

The old moon laughed and sang a song,
　　As they rocked in the wooden shoe;
And the wind that sped them all night long
　　Ruffled the waves of dew.
The little stars were the herring fish
　　That lived in the beautiful sea—
"Now cast your nets wherever you wish,
　　Never afeared are we!"
So cried the stars to the fishermen three:

　　　　　　Wynken,
　　　　　　Blynken,
　　　　　　And Nod.

All night long their nets they threw
　　For the fish in the twinkling foam,
Then down from the sky came the wooden
　　　　shoe,
　　Bringing the fishermen home;
'Twas all so pretty a sail, it seemed
　　As if it could not be;

And some folk thought 'twas a dream they'd
    dreamed
  Of sailing that beautiful sea—
But I shall name you the fishermen three:

              Wynken,
              Blynken,
              And Nod.

Wynken and Blynken are two little eyes,
  And Nod is a little head,
And the wooden shoe that sailed the skies
  Is a wee one's trundle bed;
So shut your eyes while Mother sings
  Of wonderful sights that be,
And you shall see the beautiful things,
  As you rock in the misty sea,
Where the old shoe rocked the
    fishermen three—
  Wynken, Blynken, and Nod.

                          Eugene Field

A PATTERN BABY

When people come to call and tell
About their babies, dear me, well—
I sit and listen all the while
And smile myself a little smile.
If mine were like some people's, there,
I would not keep her, I declare!
Their babies scream and cry and fret,
Won't eat or sleep, while my dear pet
She *never* cries; she'll stay for hours
Just looking at the birds and flowers.
The sweetest little cot has she,
All pink and white, as smart can be.
And when at night I lay her in it
She shuts her eyes in half a minute.
That all the babies in the city
Are not like mine I think a pity.
The only thing is, mine won't grow—
She is a baby doll, you know.

E. A. Mayo

MUSTARD AND CRESS

Elizabeth, my cousin, is the sweetest
    little girl,
From her eyes like dark blue pansies to her
    tiniest golden curl;
I do not use her great long name, but simply
    call her Bess,
And yesterday I planted her in mustard and
    in cress.

My garden is so narrow that there's very little
    room,
But I'd rather have her name than get a
    hollyhock to bloom;
And before she comes to visit us, with
    Charley and with Jess,
She'll pop up green and bonny out of mustard
    and of cress.

Norman Gale

A BOY'S SONG

Where the pools are bright and deep,
Where the grey trout lies asleep,
Up the river and over the lea,
That's the way for Billy and me.

Where the hazel bank is steepest,
Where the shadow falls the deepest,
Where the clustering nuts fall free,
That's the way for Billy and me.

Why the boys should drive away
Little sweet maidens from the play,
Or love to banter and fight so well,
That's the thing I never could tell.

But this I know, I love to play
Through the meadow, among the hay;
Up the water and over the lea,
That's the way for Billy and me.

James Hogg

THE DREAM OF A BOY WHO LIVED AT NINE-ELMS

Nine grenadiers, with bayonets in their guns;
Nine bakers' baskets, with hot cross buns;
Nine brown elephants, standing in a row;
Nine new velocipedes, good ones to go;
Nine knickerbocker suits, with buttons
    all complete;
Nine pairs of skates, with straps for the feet;
Nine clever conjurers eating hot coals;
Nine sturdy mountaineers leaping on
    their poles;
Nine little drummer boys beating on
    their drums;
Nine fat aldermen sitting on their thumbs;
Nine new knockers to our front door;
Nine new neighbours that I never saw before;
Nine times running I dreamt it all plain;
With bread and cheese for supper I could
    dream it all again.

William Brighty Rands

THE ROCK-A-BY LADY

The Rock-a-by Lady from Hushaby Street
Comes stealing, comes creeping;
The poppies they hang from her head to
    her feet,
And each hath a dream that is tiny
    and fleet—
She bringeth her poppies to you, my sweet,
When she findeth you sleeping!

Would you dream all these dreams that are
    tiny and fleet?
They'll come to you sleeping;
So shut the two eyes that are weary,
    my sweet,
For the Rock-a-by Lady from Hushaby
    Street,
With poppies that hang from her head to
    her feet,
Comes stealing; comes creeping.

Eugene Field

SEVEN TIMES ONE

There's no dew left on the daisies and clover,
    There's no rain left in heaven:
I've said my "seven times" over and over,
    Seven times one are seven.

I am old, so old I can write a letter;
    My birthday lessons are done;
The lambs play always, they know no better;
    They are only one times one.

O Columbine, open your folded wrapper,
    Where two twin turtledoves dwell!
O Cuckoopint, toll me the purple clapper
    That hangs in your clear green bell!

And show me your nest, with the young
      ones in it;
    I will not steal them away;
I am old! You may trust me, linnet, linnet,—
    I am seven times one today.

Jean Ingelow

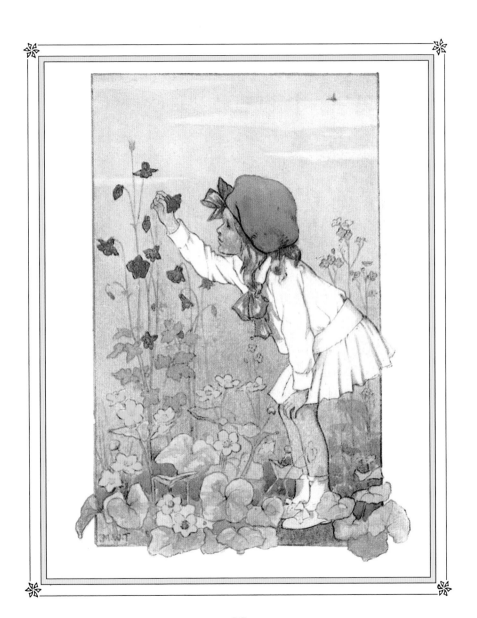

OUR VISIT TO THE ZOO

When we went to the Zoo
We saw a gnu,
An elk and a whelk
And a wild emu.

We saw a hare,
And a bear in his lair,
And a seal have a meal
On a high-backed chair.

We saw a snake
That was hardly awake,
And a lion eat meat
They'd forgotten to bake.

We saw a crab and a long-tailed dab,
And we all went home in a taxicab.

Jessie Pope

CATCHING FAIRIES

They're sleeping beneath the roses;
Oh! kiss them before they rise,
And tickle their tiny noses,
And sprinkle the dew on their eyes.
Make haste, make haste;
The fairies are caught,
Make haste.

They'll scatter sweet scents by winking,
With sparks from under their feet;
They'll save us the trouble of thinking,
Their voices will sound so sweet.
Oh stay, oh stay;
They're up and away,
Oh stay!

William Cory

THE LOST DOLL

I once had a sweet little doll, dears,
    The prettiest doll in the world;
Her cheeks were so red and so white, dears,
    And her hair was so charmingly curled.
But I lost my poor little doll, dears,
    As I played in the heath one day;
And I cried for her more than a week, dears;
    But I never could find where she lay.

I found my poor little doll, dears,
    As I played in the heath one day;
Folks say she is terribly changed, dears,
    For her paint is all washed away,
And her arm trodden off by the cows, dears,
    And her hair not the least bit curled:
Yet for old sakes' sake she is still, dears,
    The prettiest doll in the world.

Charles Kingsley

THE LOST DOLL.

A CHILD'S THOUGHT
OF GOD

They say that God lives very high!
But if you look above the pines
You cannot see our God. And why?
And if you dig down in the mines,
You never see Him in the gold,
Though from Him all that's glory shines.

God is so good, He wears a fold
Of heaven and earth across His face,
Like secrets kept, for love untold.
But still I feel that His embrace
Slides down by thrills, through all things made,
Through sight and sound of every place:

As if my tender mother laid
On my shut lids, her kisses' pressure,
Half-waking me at night; and said,
"Who kissed you in the dark, dear guesser?"

Elizabeth Barrett Browning

TARTARY

If I were Lord of Tartary,
 Myself and me alone,
My bed should be of ivory,
 Of beaten gold my throne;
And in my court should peacocks flaunt,
And in my forests tigers haunt,
And in my pools great fishes slant
 Their fins athwart the sun.

If I were Lord of Tartary,
 Trumpeters every day
To all my meals should summon me,
 And in my courtyards bray;
And in the evenings lamps should shine
Yellow as honey, red as wine,
While harp and flute and mandoline
 Made music sweet and gay.

                    Walter De La Mare

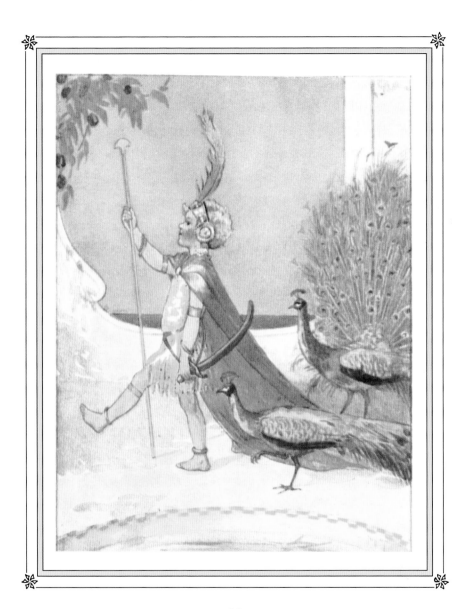

I SAW A SHIP A-SAILING

I saw a ship a-sailing,
   A-sailing on the sea;
And, oh! it was all laden
   With pretty things for thee!

There were comfits in the cabin,
   And apples in the hold;
The sails were all of silk,
   And the masts were made of gold.

Old Rhyme

AUTUMN FIRES

In the other gardens
   And all up the vale,
From the autumn bonfires
   See the smoke trail!

Pleasant summer over
   And all the summer flowers,
The red fire blazes,
   The grey smoke towers.

Sing a song of seasons!
   Something bright in all!
Flowers in the summer,
   Fires in the fall!

Robert Louis Stevenson

THE FIRST OF MAY

The fair maid who, the First of May,
   Goes to the fields at break of day,
And washes in dew from the hawthorn tree,
   Will ever after handsome be.

Old Rhyme

INFANT JOY

"I have no name;
I am but two days old."
—What shall I call thee?
"I happy am;
Joy is my name."
—Sweet joy befall thee!

Pretty joy!
Sweet joy, but two days old;
Sweet joy I call thee:
Thou dost smile:
I sing the while,
Sweet joy befall thee!

William Blake

THE MONTHS

January brings the snow,
Makes our feet and fingers glow.

February brings the rain,
Thaws the frozen lake again.

March brings breezes loud and shrill,
Stirs the dancing daffodil.

April brings the primrose sweet,
Scatters daisies at our feet.

May brings flocks of pretty lambs,
Skipping by their fleecy dams.

June brings tulips, lilies, roses,
Fills the children's hands with posies.

Hot July brings cooling showers,
Apricots and gillyflowers.

August brings the sheaves of corn,
Then the harvest home is borne.   *continued*

Warm September brings the fruit,
Sportsmen then begin to shoot.

Fresh October brings the pheasant,
Then to gather nuts is pleasant.

Dull November brings the blast,
Then the leaves are whirling fast.

Chill December brings the sleet,
Blazing fire and Christmas treat.

Sara Coleridge

OLD MOTHER GOOSE

Old Mother Goose,
   When she wanted to wander
Would ride through the air
   On a very fine gander.

Mother Goose had a house,
   'Twas built in a wood,
Where an owl at the door
   As sentinel stood.

She had a son Jack,
   A plain-looking lad,
He was not very good,
   Nor yet very bad.

She sent him to market,
   A live goose he bought;
"Here, Mother," says he,
   "It will not go for nought."

Old Rhyme

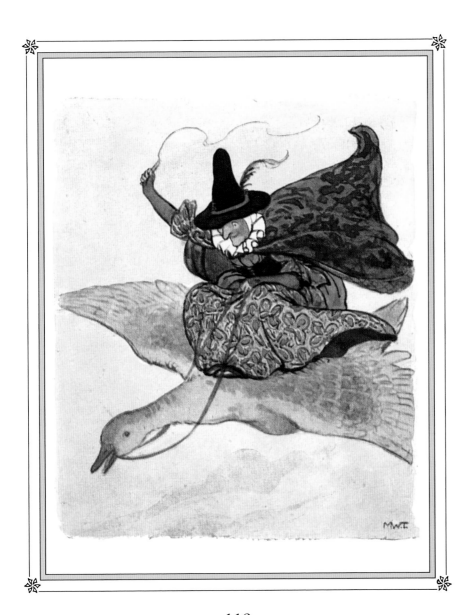

ORANGES AND LEMONS

Fast beneath the archway going
Hurry, hurry—never knowing
   When the arch will stop you!
First there comes the candle-lighting,
Then you will—it's most exciting!—
   Feel the chopper chop you!

Now we're off. Oh, hold on tight there!
Tug away with all your might there!
   Now we've nearly won it!
Lemons break, and red with laughter,
On the ground they're lying after.
   Oranges have done it!

Old Rhyme

PEG TOPS

Oh, people, please mind where you're setting
    your feet,
For peg tops are spinning all over the street,
And if they should tumble, with might and
    with main,
We have all of these tops to get spinning again.

The boys who are big will just give them
    a twirl
And all in a minute you'll see the tops whirl;
But if you are smaller, you have to begin
Quite three times or four times before they
    will spin.

Old Rhyme

A CHINESE NURSERY SONG

The mouse ran up the candlestick,
To eat the grease from off the wick.
When we got up, he could not get down,
But squeaked to waken all the town:
Ma-ma-ma! Ma-ma-ma!

From *"Cradle Songs of Many Nations"*

DAYS OF BIRTH

Monday's child is fair of face,
Tuesday's child is full of grace,
Wednesday's child is full of woe,
Thursday's child has far to go,

Friday's child is loving and giving,
Saturday's child works hard for its living,
But the child that is born on the Sabbath Day
Is fair, and wise, and good, and gay.

Old Rhyme

TUESDAY'S CHILD

WEDNESDAY'S CHILD

MONDAY'S CHILD

THURSDAY'S CHILD

SATURDAY'S CHILD

FRIDAY'S CHILD

SUNDAY'S CHILD

HERE WE GO ROUND THE MULBERRY BUSH

Here we go round the mulberry bush,
  The mulberry bush, the mulberry bush,
Here we go round the mulberry bush,
  So early in the morning.

This is the way we wash our hands,
Wash our hands, wash our hands,
This is the way we wash our hands
  So early in the morning.

This is the way we go to school,
Go to school, go to school,
This is the way we go to school
  So early in the morning.

Old Rhyme

123

THE <u>PEDLAR'S CARAVAN</u>

I wish I lived in a caravan,
With a horse to drive, like a pedlar-man!
Where he comes from nobody knows,
Or where he goes to, but on he goes!

His caravan has windows two,
And a chimney of tin, that the smoke
   comes through;
He has a wife with a baby brown,
And they go a-riding from town to town.

Chairs to mend, and delft to sell!
He clashes the basins like a bell;
Tea trays, baskets ranged in order,
Plates, with alphabets round the border!

The roads are brown, and the sea is green,
But his house is like a bathing-machine;
The world is round, and he can ride,
Rumble and splash, to the other side!

continued

With the pedlar-man I should like to roam,
And write a book when I came home;
All the people would read my book,
Just like the Travels of Captain Cook!

William Brighty Rands

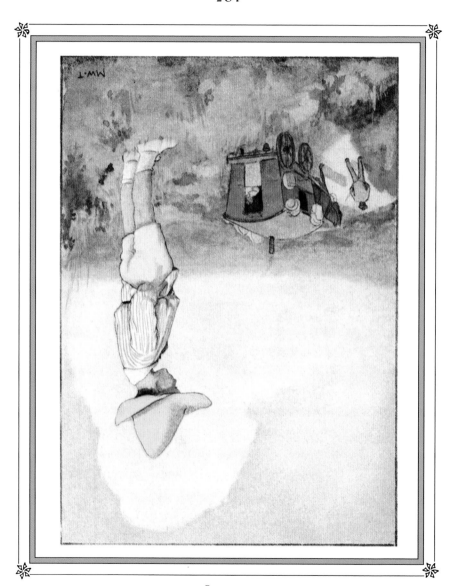